I0526892

What's in the Rømmegrøt?!

What's in the Rømmegrøt?!

A Family Food Foible

By Carol Hagen

Illustrated by
Kari Vick
with Betty Dowe

Penfield
BOOKS

Cover by MACook Design
Layout Editor: Deb Schense
Printed in the U.S.A.

Penfield Books
215 Brown Street
Iowa City, IA 52245
1-319-337-9998
www.penfieldbooks.com

ISBN-13: 978-1572161252
© 2020 Carol Hagen

For Haaken,
Hannah and Adam,
Cora and Maeve,
and all Rømmegrøt eaters!

~

For Ella and Heather,
Alice and Christine…
who also love lefse.

"Let's have rømmegrøt for breakfast!" shouted Ella, bounding down the stairs one white wintery morning at Grandma's house.

"Good idea, Ella!" replied Grandma. "What a perfect morning to warm up with rømmegrøt"...

...and she started rattling pans in the kitchen.

And she got out milk,

sugar,

butter,

flour,

and salt

to make the sweet, creamy porridge.

Ella slid a stool over to the cupboard, grabbed two bowls,
then climbed down and pulled two spoons from a drawer.

Meanwhile, Grandma scalded milk on the stove, and

S   L   O   W   L   Y

melted butter in a pan.

They added flour to the butter,
poured in hot milk,
shook in a dash of salt,
tossed in a bit of sugar,
then...

Whisk!... whisk!...

whisked it all together,

Grandma's firm hand aswirl!

Soon, the porridge was *plop, pop, glopping...*
thick bubbles breaking the surface.

Off to the side, Grandma mixed
up the best part of all—

cinnamon and sugar
to go on top!

15

Ella's mouth watered as she found her seat at the table, gripping her spoon in wait.

Pan in hand,
    Grandma dished up two servings
        of thick rømmegrøt into the bowls.

She sprinkled a generous amount of cinnamon-sugar on top.

A dollop of butter was the final touch.
Mmmmmm...Ella couldn't wait!

She scooped a big spoonful and gave
it a taste. So did Grandma.

"Eeewwwww!"
they both cried.

"Something's not right!"
exclaimed Grandma.

"This tastes weird,"
Ella agreed.

What
could
be
wrong?!

Grandma leapt from
her chair and sprang
to the other side
of the kitchen,
her eyes
roaming the
counter.
Resting her gaze on
a small square jar,
she sighed,
"Uff Da!
I must have
put *garlic* in
the rømmegrøt!"

*"**Garlic** in the rømmegrøt?"* Ella's eyes were wide.

"Why did you do that, Grandma?"

"I made a mistake," Grandma admitted. "The garlic powder jar looks just like the cinnamon jar. I must have grabbed it by mistake and mixed it with the sugar.

"I am sorry, Ella. This tastes awful."

Ella made her way to the stove and saw the pan of rømmegrøt still on top. She wondered, "Is there still some left?"

Grandma came beside her and peered into the pan. "Why, yes, there is still some left!"

"You didn't put the garlic on until it was in the bowls,"
Ella reminded her, "so what's left should still be alright,
shouldn't it, Grandma?"

"You're right, Ella. This time, we'll put *real* cinnamon and sugar on,"
and she found a *different* small square jar, opened it carefully
and sniffed . . . . just to make sure.
"Mmmmm- –here, you smell, Ella. Does this
smell like cinnamon?"

Ella stuck her nose into the jar and took a big sniff. **"Hachew!!!"**
she sneezed. "Yup, that's cinnamon, Grandma."

Then they each ate a small bowl of rømmegrøt
with cinnamon, sugar, and butter on top.

And they both felt warm, full, and happy.

The End

Rømmegrøt is a thick, simple porridge made by early Norwegian immigrants to the U.S., many settling in the upper Midwestern states. The author's great grandparents immigrated to the U.S. from Norway in the late 1800s, and rømmegrøt was often made in their, and their descendents' homes.

The author made rømmegrøt as a treat for her children, and now, makes it for her grandchildren, especially at Christmas. She makes a "citified" version, using milk and butter, instead of cream or sour cream which was used in old Norway. Here is the recipe (and be sure to use cinnamon, NOT garlic powder!):

City Rømmegrøt*

1 quart milk, scalded   1 teaspoon salt
1/2 cup butter (or margarine) 5 tablespoon sugar
1 cup flour   Cinnamon

Melt butter or margarine in a heavy pan. Add 1 cup flour slowly as when making cream sauce. Watch carefully so that it doesn't scorch. Add scalded milk a little at a time. Mix and beat until smooth and thick. Add salt and sugar. Mix and pour into serving dish or bowls. Sprinkle more sugar and cinnamon on top and a little melted butter. Enjoy!

*From **Notably Norwegian** later **Norwegian Touches** revised and expanded. Page 149. Penfield Books (www.penfieldbooks.com) Reprinted with permission.

Rosemaling is a traditional decorative folk art that began in the rural valleys of Norway. Rosemaling uses flowers, scroll-work and geometric shapes in flowing patterns. Can you find all the examples of rosemaling in this book?

Try your hand at rosemaling, too! You may color the images on the next page, or make photocopies of the page to try different color combinations.

Designs by Betty Dowe, creator of *Strokes of Love* coloring book. (rosemalingbybettydowe.com).
Permission to photocopy for personal use only.

31

The Author

Carol Hagen lives in Decorah, Iowa with her husband, Eddy, and cat, Savannah, in an old pink house where many food foibles have unfolded. This is her first children's book.

The Illustrator

On the north shore of Lake Superior, Kari Vick gardens with her husband, Jim and often gathers with daughters, Kjersti and Solveig, to fish, forage…and feast upon seasonal delights.

www.ingramcontent.com/pod-product-compliance
Lightning Source LLC
Chambersburg PA
CBHW041720240626

47171CB00002B/17